Pellie Runs A Marathon

To
Brooke~
Someday you'll
"run right to it" with your
own little
runner~
Michele
Brodia
Graeber

For Patrick & Will, 2 little boys who love to
run right to it! - MBC

For Mom & Dad, for teaching me
to never give up. -EL

Thank you, Saucony, for your shared vision
in a healthier future for children.

power pack presentations
PO Box 747
Upton, MA 01568-0747
www.powerpackpresentations.com

10 9 8 7 6 5 4 3 2 1
Library of Congress Control Number: 2003091226
ISBN 0-9740130-0-5

Printed in Canada.

This book is available at quantity discounts. - Great for use at
race expos, trade shows, health fairs and as incentives or prizes.
Please contact power pack presentations for more information.

Pellie Runs A Marathon

by Michele Bredice Craemer

illustrated by Elizabeth Lavin

power pack presentations
Massachusetts

Pellie runs a marathon -

26.2 miles.

Let's go with her,
through the work
& the smiles.

At mile 1,

A little girl cheers,
"Smile, Pellie, smile!"

And Pellie begins to run –
mile after mile.

Right at mile 2,

Sammie runs past Pellie.

But a few steps later,
Pellie runs in front of Ellie.

It's mile 3 & 4.

There is a big laughing hill.

Pellie knows she can slow
down a bit,
as long as she doesn't
stand still!

At miles 5 & 6,

Pellie's feeling fine.

Her heart is pumping
and her feathers begin to shine.

Look at mile 8.

A big tree is in the way.

Pellie trips and falls,
then starts to run again.
Hurray!

At miles 14 & 15,

Pellie looks to the crowd.

As she puffs and puffs,
they all cheer out loud.

At miles 16 & 17,

Pellie's feet begin to slow.

But running feels like swinging.
She wants to go, go, go!

It's miles 18, 19 & 20.

Pellie runs into "the wall"!

It is big & she is shocked.
But then she runs –
that's all!

It's mile 25

and it's almost over.

It feels like finding
a 4 leaf clover!

25m

Pellie finishes the
marathon!

It's such a happy feeling
that will go on & on!

In 26.2 miles, Pellie learned:

Enjoy the race
Run at your own pace

Enjoy today
Hills are okay

Run through it
Run right to it

Enjoy the work
The race is a perk

See yourself getting there
It all starts here!

About the Author

The adventures of Pellie are based on the author's true experiences of training for and running marathons.

Michele presents seminars on wellness and motivation. This is her first book. She lives in Massachusetts with her husband and 2 young sons.

About the Illustrator

Elizabeth is a freelance photographer and illustrator. Her other works include *Jack Straw: A Halloween Mystery*. She lives in Narragansett, Rhode Island where she is looking for her next adventure.